Barbie
— AS —
Rapunzel
A Junior Novelization

Adapted by Kimberly Weinberger

Based on the script by
Elana Lesser & Cliff Ruby

SCHOLASTIC INC.
New York   Toronto   London   Auckland   Sydney
Mexico City   New Delhi   Hong Kong   Buenos Aires

ISBN 0-439-44295-8

Designed by Peter Koblish
Photography by Willy Lew, Laura Lynch, Lin Carlson, Jennifer Hoon, Analyn Mori, Jake Johnson, Keith Biele, Krista Borden, Scott Meskill, Steve Toth, Lisa Collins, and Judy Tsuno

12 11 10 9 8 7 6 5 4 3   2 3 4 5 6 7/0

Printed in the U.S.A.
First Scholastic printing, September 2002

Introduction

It was a time of castles, kings, magic, and dragons. In a dark forest, a secret manor stood surrounded by gardens. A magic wall made the manor invisible to all who passed near it . . . and kept a young girl hidden inside.

Her name was Rapunzel, and she was as kind as she was beautiful. Long blond hair flowed like a river down her back. Day after day, she lived within the walls of her magic prison. But all of that was about to change. . . .

Chapter 1
A Secret Room

"Look at this," said Penelope. The purple dragon's tail flopped behind her. "I mean, look at this painting. I can *smell* the salt water. I can *feel* the mist!"

Rapunzel laughed. "One day I'm going to walk along a beach just like this one," said Rapunzel.

But her daydream quickly ended. The sound of a galloping horse echoed outside.

"Gothel alert!" shouted Hobie. The rabbit's ears turned this way and that.

He and Penelope were Rapunzel's only

friends in the world. They both tried their best to protect her from the evil witch, Gothel.

Rapunzel raced into the entrance hall as Gothel arrived. "I'll expect my tea in nine minutes," the witch snapped.

"Yes, my lady," the girl replied.

"What's that?" Gothel asked, staring at Rapunzel's face.

Rapunzel put her hand to her cheek. There was a streak of paint there.

"Painting again? What about your chores?" Gothel asked.

"I — I finished them," Rapunzel answered nervously.

"Hmph," said Gothel. "I must not be giving you enough to do." With that, she swept away.

Rapunzel's list of chores was endless:

sweep the floors, weed the garden, beat the rugs, polish the silver, wash Gothel's clothes, and, of course, make her tea.

Penelope and Hobie joined Rapunzel in the kitchen. "I hope Gothel chokes on her tea," Hobie muttered.

"Now, Hobie," Rapunzel said. She tried not to think bad thoughts about Gothel. Af-

ter all, Gothel had taken her in when she was abandoned at just a few days old.

Rapunzel carried the tea tray to the door. Penelope ran after her with a lemon. As usual, the dragon forgot that she was too big to run in such a small room. She crashed into the tray, sending it sailing into the air.

The three friends used every hand, tail,

and paw they had to catch the flying tea set. Only one cup got away. It fell onto a ladle, which flew across the room and landed on a carved dragon's head over the fireplace.

The dragon's head tilted forward, and a secret panel slid quietly open. Behind the panel lay a staircase.

"I wonder where it goes?" Rapunzel whispered. She started down the stairs.

"What about the tea?" asked Hobie.

"We still have a few minutes. Come on."

Penelope and Hobie followed close behind her.

The friends found themselves in a dusty storeroom. It was filled with old papers and boxes. Rapunzel discovered a wooden chest in a corner.

"What a lovely old box," she murmured, lifting the lid. Inside lay a delicate silver hairbrush. Rapunzel read the words that were written on the back:

Constant as the stars above,
always know that you are loved.
To our daughter, Rapunzel,
on her first birthday.
With love forever,
Mother and Father.

Rapunzel frowned. "Gothel said I was abandoned when I was a few days old," she said. "Why would she lie to me about that?"

Just then, Gothel called for her tea. Rapunzel hurried upstairs. She returned to the secret room a few minutes later. Hobie and Penelope were still there.

"I see a big, hairy spider!" cried Hobie.

Penelope squealed and jumped away. Her foot crashed straight through the floor.

"Hmmm," Rapunzel said. "That's funny. . . ."

She and Penelope and Hobie peered into the hole Penelope had made. They

were surprised to see a long tunnel beneath them.

Rapunzel lowered herself through the opening. She was scared, but she knew she had to follow that tunnel, wherever it might lead. This might be her only chance to go outside the magic wall.

"I'll be back soon," she said.

"We'll be here," said Hobie. "Worrying."

Chapter 2
Beyond the Magic Wall

Rapunzel followed the rocky tunnel until she saw a faint light. Taking a deep breath, she squeezed through a small opening. Before her lay a beautiful, bustling village.

Rapunzel had never seen anything like the village before. She wandered around in wonder. The sights and smells dazzled her. Soon she came to a lush garden at the foot of an enormous castle.

Three young girls played near an apple tree. Rapunzel watched as they talked and laughed. Suddenly, one of the girls fell through a hole hidden by a patch of leaves.

"Help me!" cried the child.

Rapunzel raced to the edge of the hole. She reached for the girl and pulled her to her side.

"You're all right now," said Rapunzel.

At that moment, the dirt under Rapunzel's feet gave way. For a terrifying second,

she felt herself falling. Then two strong hands pulled Rapunzel and the child to safety.

Rapunzel looked up at the handsome young man who had helped her.

"Thank you for saving my sister," he said.

"And thank you," replied Rapunzel, "for saving me."

The young man hugged his sister, then sent her over to her friends. "Have we met before?" he asked Rapunzel.

"I've . . . I've never been here before," Rapunzel replied.

The young man looked concerned. "Do you live in Wilhelm's kingdom?"

"Who's he?" asked Rapunzel.

"He's the one who ordered *that*," the young man said, pointing at the pit.

"Why would he do such an awful thing?" asked Rapunzel.

"You don't know? Wilhelm says our king did something terrible to him years ago."

"Did he?" asked Rapunzel.

"No!" the young man exclaimed.

"Then can't the two kings talk it over?" asked Rapunzel.

"It's too late now. The only way to make things better is to fight," explained the young man.

"That seems foolish," said Rapunzel.

The young man smiled. "Oh, you think so?" Just then, they could hear the girls giggling and shouting. "I better make sure they're all right. I'll be right back," he said.

Just then, Rapunzel realized the time.

She had stayed too long! When the young man returned, she was gone.

Rapunzel reached the entrance to the tunnel just as the sun began to set. She slipped through the rocky opening and hurried down the path.

A small figure moved just as quickly behind Rapunzel. It was Otto, Gothel's sly ferret. He liked to spy on Rapunzel and make trouble for her. He followed the girl back to the manor, laughing to himself all the way.

14

Chapter 3
The Silver Paintbrush

"Tell me again about the village," said Penelope. "And don't leave anything out."

Rapunzel was back in her small room, telling her friends about her adventure. "You should see it," said Rapunzel, her eyes shining. "The people, the castle, the food. But the best part was . . . I met somebody. He was kind and strong and —"

"What was his name?" Penelope asked.

"I don't know," said Rapunzel, surprising herself. "I didn't even ask."

Suddenly, Hobie's long ears began to

turn. He had barely squeaked, "Gothel alert!" before the witch burst in.

"Did we have a nice little trip today?" Gothel demanded.

Rapunzel stood still, shocked. Then she saw Otto on Gothel's shoulder. "Otto," she whispered to herself, realizing what he'd done.

"After all I've done, this is how you repay me? By sneaking off?" Gothel demanded.

"But I — why didn't you tell me about the village? It's so close by," Rapunzel stammered.

"I did it to protect you from the evil there," said Gothel.

"But everyone was so kind," Rapunzel protested.

"Yes, I heard you met someone special," Gothel said in an icy tone. "Who was he?"

"I — I don't know his name," Rapunzel stammered.

"Liar!" shouted Gothel.

"I'm telling the truth," Rapunzel said.

But Gothel didn't believe her. Rapunzel

watched in horror as Gothel destroyed her paints and all of her beautiful paintings.

"Why are you doing this?" Rapunzel cried. "You can't lock me away forever!"

"Watch me," said Gothel.

And with that, a blue glow exploded from the witch. The door to the room disappeared. The stair vanished. The walls stretched until they were four stories high.

The room had become a tower — and a prison with no escape.

Gothel turned to go. "Hugo!" she called. A huge dragon swooped down from the sky. He was Penelope's father and Gothel's loyal servant.

Gothel climbed onto the dragon's back. "Make sure Rapunzel stays put," Gothel commanded. "Or else . . ." She shot an electric spark at him as a warning.

That night, Rapunzel dreamed of the young man from the village. He called to her from the grounds outside the tower.

Rapunzel let her long blond hair tumble out of the small window. The young man easily climbed up.

But even in her dreams, Rapunzel could not escape from Gothel. The witch ap-

peared in the form of a giant. She snatched Rapunzel away from the young man.

Rapunzel awoke with a start. She pulled out the gleaming silver hairbrush.

"'Constant as the stars above,'" she whispered, "'always know that you are loved. . . .'"

The words made her feel strong.

"I'm going to be free," she vowed.

As Rapunzel drifted back to sleep, a bright star shot across the night sky. Its magical light fell on the silver hairbrush. In a shower of sparkles, the hairbrush turned into a beautiful paintbrush.

Rapunzel slept on.

The next day, Penelope and Hobie gathered berries to make red paint for Rapunzel. Penelope flew to the tower window with Hobie on her back.

Rapunzel was touched by the thoughtful gift. "I don't know what to say!"

"Uh-oh," said Penelope. "We forgot a paintbrush."

Hobie picked up the silver paintbrush from the window ledge.

"What about this one?" he asked.

Rapunzel was confused. The brush had the same words on it as her hairbrush had. But how had it become a paintbrush?

She dipped the brush into the red paint and touched it to the dreary tower wall. The paint turned to a lovely sky blue!

"How did you do that?" Penelope asked.

"I don't know," said Rapunzel. "I was thinking of the blue sky, and there it was!"

Rapunzel began to paint. Soon the room was filled with incredible scenes of the village and the great castle. It was like magic! The butterflies and birds in the picture almost seemed to move.

Then Penelope accidentally pushed Hobie against the wall. To everyone's surprise, his head went right through the painting!

Rapunzel and Penelope quickly pulled him back into the tower. Then Rapunzel put her hand through the painting, wondering. Could it be a magical doorway to the village itself?

Rapunzel knew she had to find out. She hugged her friends good-bye. Then she bravely walked into the painting and disappeared.

Chapter 4
The Invitation

With a shimmering sparkle, Rapunzel suddenly found herself in the garden of the village's castle. It had worked! She was free. And there was the young man she had met the day before. He jumped up to greet her.

"I hoped you might come back here," he said eagerly. "I realized I don't even know your name."

Rapunzel told the young man her name. But she stopped him from telling her his own. She didn't want Gothel to find out who he was.

"Can you help me find the maker of this

brush?" Rapunzel asked. She held out her silver paintbrush. Perhaps whoever made it would know something about her parents.

"Let's start with the silversmith," said the young man.

The silversmith knew right away who had made the brush — his brother.

"That's wonderful!" said Rapunzel. "May I speak with him?"

"I'm afraid not," the silversmith said sadly. "I haven't spoken with him myself in years."

The silversmith explained that because of the fight between the two kingdoms, the people of both kingdoms were not allowed to see one another.

"You must miss him," said Rapunzel.

When she turned to her friend, she saw that he looked even sadder than the silversmith. Had the feud hurt him as well?

Meanwhile, trouble was on its way to the tower. Penelope and Hobie watched as Gothel stormed across the garden.

Penelope began to panic. Her father, the fearsome dragon Hugo, was supposed to be guarding the tower. What would Gothel do to him if she discovered Rapunzel had escaped?

Penelope was scared, but she decided to go after Rapunzel. She took a deep breath and leaped into the painting.

Meanwhile, Rapunzel and the young man were strolling through the garden. "I'm sorry you didn't find out more about your parents," said the young man.

"I'm not giving up," said Rapunzel.

"Good. Um, I was wondering if . . ." He pulled a scroll out of his pocket and handed it to her.

"You are herewith invited to the masked ball in honor of the prince's birthday," Rapunzel read. She looked at the young man and smiled. "You must be pretty important if you're invited to the prince's ball."

"Oh, I don't know about that," the young man replied, blushing. "Will you come?"

"I'd love to," Rapunzel answered.

At that moment, Penelope appeared. "Rapunzel!" she called.

The young man was alarmed to see a dragon. He drew his sword to protect Rapunzel.

"Wait!" Rapunzel cried. "She's my friend."

"You're friends with a dragon?" the young man said, surprised.

"Rapunzel! You have to come with me. Gothel's coming!" Penelope exclaimed. "If she finds out you're gone, she'll do something terrible to my father."

Rapunzel nodded. She turned back to the young man. "I have to go. But I will see you tonight. I'll explain everything then." She and Penelope hurried away.

Rapunzel stopped quickly at the garden's gate. She used her magic brush to paint a picture of the tower. "I hope this works," she whispered, grabbing Penelope's claw. They jumped through the gate and into the painting, disappearing in a flash.

The two made it back to the tower just in

time. Gothel did not know they had been gone. Penelope's father was safe, for now.

Later that afternoon, Rapunzel used her paintbrush to create her dress for the ball. She painted frilly dresses and simple ones, modern dresses and old-fashioned ones.

Finally, she created the perfect gown. Penelope and Hobie helped by making a mask. By sunset, Rapunzel was ready. But Gothel had other plans for her.

Rapunzel and her friends were too busy to notice Gothel's ferret. Otto crept into the tower room and watched Rapunzel trying on the dresses. Then he saw the invitation to the ball on Rapunzel's table. He silently snatched it and scurried off to Gothel.

Gothel arrived in the tower room just as Rapunzel was about to leave.

"You do look lovely in your party clothes," the witch sneered. "But your hair is not quite right."

With a bolt of magic, Gothel chopped off Rapunzel's beautiful locks. Then she destroyed the magic painting on the wall and the silver paintbrush.

"One more chance, Rapunzel," she said. "Who is the young man? Tell me his name."

"I don't know," Rapunzel said truthfully.

"Then live with your lies forever!" cried the witch. She began to chant: *"Tower, tower, do your part. Never release your prisoner with the lying heart. Note that as these words are spoken, this fearsome spell can never be broken!"*

An eerie blue light fell over the tower. Poor Rapunzel was trapped — again.

Chapter 5
The Masked Ball

Gothel arrived at the ball with Rapunzel's invitation in hand. She hid her face behind a fancy mask. A wig made from Rapunzel's beautiful hair covered her head.

The witch stepped onto the dance floor in search of Rapunzel's young man. A voice called out to her.

"Rapunzel?" It was the handsome young man. Gothel realized that he was the king's son, Prince Stefan. Her trap had worked! Now she would lure him away from the party.

Gothel hurried through the castle gardens and into a maze of hedges. She waited for the prince.

"Ah," Prince Stefan said when he caught up to her. "The masked lady finally stops."

As the young man smiled at her, Gothel lowered her mask. Stefan realized she was not Rapunzel after all.

"Who are you?" he demanded.

"I'm the one who's going to teach you not to meddle with my plans," Gothel growled. She threw a bolt of magic at him.

As Prince Stefan fought against the evil witch, Rapunzel paced inside her stone prison. She just had to find a way out. But how?

The answer came from an unlikely

friend. At the bottom of the tower stood Hugo. Penelope was begging him to help Rapunzel. But the fierce dragon refused.

Then Penelope told him how Rapunzel had saved his life.

"She was free," said Penelope tearfully. "She came back so Gothel wouldn't destroy you."

The dragon realized that he had to help Rapunzel. "I wish there was something I could do. But spells are unbreakable."

The dragon tried to use his flaming breath to destroy the spell on the tower. Then he remembered the words the witch had spoken.

"The spell only traps a prisoner with a *lying* heart," Hugo said slowly.

Penelope began to smile.

"But Rapunzel isn't a liar!" she cried.

Penelope wasted no time. She flew to Rapunzel's window and explained the plan.

Rapunzel looked nervously at the glowing blue wall. If Hugo was wrong, she wasn't sure what would happen to her!

Rapunzel gathered all of her courage. She jumped through the window and landed

neatly on Penelope's back. The glowing wall had not harmed her.

"Thank you, Hugo!" she called.

"It is I who must thank you," the dragon replied.

Hobie joined Rapunzel and Penelope. The three said good-bye to Hugo, and Penelope flew them into the air. She soared over the magic wall, heading straight for the masked ball.

Chapter 6
The Truth Is Told

The battle between Gothel and Prince Stefan raged on. The prince tried to defend himself against the witch's magic. The two fought their way through the castle, ending up in the ballroom. But when they entered the hall, they saw another battle taking place there.

Prince Stefan's father, King Frederick, stood before his greatest enemy. It was King Wilhelm, ruler of the neighboring kingdom. King Wilhelm had come to the ball to destroy his enemy. But the sight of Gothel stopped him.

"Gothel? Is that you?" Wilhelm said to the witch.

"You know her?" Prince Stefan asked. "Who is she?"

King Wilhelm explained that he and Gothel were once friends, many years ago.

"Friends?!" cried Gothel. "You loved me. I know you did."

"No," said Wilhelm. "I never loved you."

"And for that, you will pay once again!" Gothel cried, aiming a bolt at the king.

Wilhelm fell to the ground. Then he staggered up again. "Pay again? What are you talking about?"

Gothel turned to King Frederick. "Let me ask you, Frederick, why do you hate this man?"

"He attacked my kingdom without cause," declared King Frederick.

King Wilhelm glared at him. "I attacked your kingdom because you kidnapped my daughter!"

"No!" cried King Frederick. "I never kidnapped her!"

"Lies!" King Wilhelm replied. "I know you did."

"No," said Gothel. "*I* did."

"What?" cried King Wilhelm.

"She would have been *my* daughter if you had married *me*," Gothel said. "I simply took what was mine."

King Wilhelm's eyes filled with tears. All these years he had thought that King Frederick had taken Rapunzel. "Where is she?"

"What does it matter? You'll never see her again," Gothel replied scornfully.

"I've seen her," Prince Stefan said softly.

"Where? When?" whispered King Wilhelm.

"I'm finished with you. I hate you all!" The witch lifted her hand and pointed it straight at King Wilhelm's heart.

"No!" cried a voice.

It was Rapunzel. She, Penelope, and Hobie dashed into the room. They stood bravely before Gothel.

"Impossible!" cried Gothel.

"You kept me locked up my entire life because you hated my father?" Rapunzel asked.

"He deserved to suffer as I did!" Gothel declared.

"No more suffering, Gothel. Not for anyone," Rapunzel said.

"You think you can stop me?" sneered the witch. "You and your friends won't live to see the next sunrise."

Gothel raised her arms. Rapunzel had nowhere to run.

Suddenly, a chair slid across the room, knocking Gothel over. Prince Stefan had saved Rapunzel, at least for a short time.

"Run, Rapunzel!" cried the prince.

Rapunzel knew exactly where to go. She raced toward the castle garden and stopped at the gate. The tower Rapunzel had painted there still loomed behind it. The girl stood her ground against the witch.

"Please, Gothel, we can all start over. I

forgive you for all those years," said the
girl. "No more hatred, please."

But Gothel wouldn't listen. She rushed
toward Rapunzel, who ran through the garden gate. When Gothel followed, she fell
directly into the painting and into the
tower.

Gothel's own curse sealed her fate. She
was a liar, and the tower would never let her

escape. She would be trapped there forever.

Rapunzel and her friends flew back to the grand ballroom. There Rapunzel met her father, King Wilhelm, for the very first time.

"Your mother and I have never stopped thinking about you," the king said tearfully. "Our love is as constant . . ."

". . . as the stars above," said Rapunzel.

King Wilhelm hugged his daughter. Then he turned to King Frederick.

"I've wronged you all these years," he said. "I'm more sorry than words can say."

King Frederick offered his hand to King Wilhelm. Their long feud was finally over.

Rapunzel turned to Prince Stefan, who hugged her. "Are you all right?"

Rapunzel smiled up at him. "I am now."

Rapunzel and Prince Stefan were married a short time later. The people in both kingdoms gathered to wish them well, including the silversmith and his brother!

The couple began their new life in a castle by the sea. Penelope, Hobie, and Hugo lived there, too. Rapunzel walked along the beach every day, just as she had dreamed not so long ago.

With Prince Stefan and her family and friends by her side, all her dreams had come true.